TESSA KRAILING

The Petsitters Club
10. The Rude Parrot

Illustrated by Jan Lewis

BARRON'S

First edition for the United States, Canada, and the Philippines published by
Barron's Educational Series, Inc., 1999.

First published in Great Britain in 1999 by Scholastic Children's Books,
Commonswealth House, 1-19 New Oxford Street, London WC1A 1NU, UK
A division of Scholastic Ltd

All inquiries should be addressed to:

Barron's Educational Series, Inc.
250 Wireless Boulevard
Hauppauge, New York 11788

ISBN 0-7641-1193-0
Library of Congress Catalog Card No. 99-64891

Printed in United States of America
9 8 7 6 5 4 3 2 1

Chapter 1

A Box of Chocolates

The doorbell rang. Mom called out, "Matthew, see who that is, please. I'm busy."

Matthew sighed. He pressed the pause button on the video and went to the front door. His friend Ryan Bates stood on the doorstep, holding a large square object covered by a checkered tablecloth.

"Hi, Ryan," said Matthew. "What have you got there?"

"A parrot." Ryan lifted the cloth to reveal a birdcage. "His name's Alfie. Can the Petsitters look after him, please?"

Matthew stared at the large gray bird with a short red tail and curious, light yellow eyes. "He's not a very brightly colored parrot," he said.

"He's an African Grey," said Ryan.

Matthew didn't know much about looking after parrots. Nor did the other Petsitters. "It's funny you've never mentioned him before," he said. "How long have you had him?"

"About three months." Ryan dropped the cloth back over the cage. "But now my mom's got a friend coming to stay, and she doesn't want Alfie in the house while she's here."

"Why not?" asked Matthew. "Doesn't your mom's friend like parrots?"

"I don't know." Ryan turned rather pink. "Can you look after him? It's only for a week."

"We-ell," said Matthew reluctantly, "I suppose, if you give us instructions—"

"Thanks!" Ryan thrust the cage at Matthew. "I'll get the rest of his stuff. My mom's waiting in the car outside."

He raced down the front path. Seconds later he returned with a bag and a T-shaped perch on a stand.

"You can put this in a corner of your living room." He handed the perch to Matthew. "Alfie doesn't like being stuck in his cage. There's enough food in the bag for a week, and I've written down everything he needs on a piece of paper. His special treat is corn-on-the-cob. Oh, and here's a box of chocolates."

Matthew stared at the enormous gold box tied with red ribbon. "The parrot eats *chocolates*?"

"No, they're for your mother. My mom sent them especially for her." Ryan started backing away. "Bye, Matthew."

"Wait a minute," said Matthew. "I forgot to ask. Does he talk?"

Ryan turned pink again. "Sometimes. But if you put him back in his cage and keep it covered, he usually shuts up. Bye."

He raced down the path. The car drove off quickly.

Matthew left the T-shaped stand on the porch, together with the carrier bag. He carried the cage and the box of chocolates into the kitchen.

Mom sat at the table, writing an essay for her college course. "Who was it?" she asked without looking up.

"Ryan Bates," said Matthew. "He's a friend of mine from school."

The kitchen table was covered with books. Matthew cleared a corner and set down the cage.

Mom still didn't look up. "What did he want?"

"He brought you these." Matthew gave her the chocolates. "They're a present from his mother."

Mom stared at the gold box. "But I've never met Mrs. Bates. Why should she send me chocolates?"

"I'm not sure," Matthew admitted. "I think it's to thank us for looking after her parrot."

"Her *parrot!*" At last Mom noticed the cage. "Oh, it's one of your petsitting jobs. But in that case, the chocolates must be for you, not me."

Matthew shook his head. "Ryan definitely said they were for you."

"How strange!" Mom reached for the box and untied the ribbon. "But how very, very delicious!"

On the following day, Jovan sat in his garden, staring gloomily at a large glass tank. Inside the tank was a lot of green stuff and one small brown spotted toad. "It's no use," he sighed to himself. "I don't like toads. I'm sorry he got hurt in an accident, and I hope he gets better soon. But I just – don't – like – him."

"Hi, Jo," said two voices behind him.

Startled, Jovan turned around to see Matthew with his young sister Katie.

"Oh, hello," he said. "What have you got there?" He pointed to a large square object covered with a checkered tablecloth.

"It's a parrot." Matthew lifted the cloth just long enough for Jovan to see a large gray bird with a short red tail. "His name's Alfie."

"Ryan Bates asked us to look after him," said Katie. "But our mom says she doesn't want him in the house, so we brought him to you."

"It's only for a week," said Matthew. "Well, six days now."

"We've brought all his food and everything." Katie held out a bag filled with things. "His favorite treat is corn-on-the-cob. But I warn you, he spits the bits out everywhere."

"And we've left his perch outside your front door," said Matthew.

"Why doesn't your mom want him in the house?" asked Jovan, puzzled.

Matthew looked embarrassed. "I don't think she likes him much. But your mother likes animals, so she probably won't mind, especially if you give her these chocolates. They're from Ryan." He held out an enormous gold box tied with red ribbon.

"We've eaten four," said Katie. "But there's plenty left."

Jovan stared at the cage. He didn't much like caged birds, especially parrots with big curved beaks that looked as if they could peck your eyes out.

"I'm pretty busy right now," he said. "My dad's given me this toad to look after. It was hurt in a road accident, and someone brought it into his office."

Katie peered into the tank. "Oh, he's beautiful! Has he got a name?"

"No, he's just a toad." Jovan had an idea. "Look, why don't we do a swap? If you'll look after this toad, I'll look after your parrot."

"I'd love to look after him!" Katie looked delighted. "I will call him Mr. Toad. You know, like Toad of Toad Hall."

Jovan gave her the tank. "Dad says he's only suffering from shock. As soon as he starts jumping around again, you can release him back into the wild."

"Here's Alfie." Matthew thrust the birdcage at Jovan. "If you get fed up with his talking, you can put him back in his cage and cover it with the cloth."

Katie giggled. "It doesn't always shut him up, though."

Matthew gave her a warning nudge. "Don't listen to her," he told Jovan. "Alfie's a nice bird, really he is. Bye, Jo."

Jovan watched them go. Then he carried the cage – and the chocolates – inside to show his mother.

Chapter 2

Aunt Cynthia

Sam woke up with the feeling that something had happened. For a moment she couldn't remember what it was. Then it all came back to her.

AUNT CYNTHIA HAD COME TO VISIT!

She wasn't really Sam's aunt, she was Sam's father's aunt, which meant she was pretty ancient. "A nice old bat," was how

Dad described her, "but a terrible fusspot." And sure enough, within minutes of arriving, Aunt Cynthia had spotted dust under the hall cupboard and a cobweb hanging from the ceiling.

"Really, George!" she tutted. "Still having cleaning problems, I see? I've always said this house is much too big for just the two of you."

Sam groaned and pulled the quilt over her head. Last time Aunt Cynthia had come to visit, she had been frightened by a garter snake the Petsitters were looking after. At least this time there were no pets in the house. No snakes, no goats, no rats. So *this* time she'd have no cause for complaint.

Sam got dressed and went downstairs. She found her father in the kitchen, heating water.

"I thought I'd take Aunt Cynthia a cup of tea in bed," he said. "Try to put the old bat in a good mood for the day."

"Dad!" Sam giggled.

He sighed. "I'm fond of her, you know I am. She's basically very kindhearted. But I wish she wouldn't find fault with everything."

"Especially your work." Sam put on a disapproving, Aunt Cynthia-type voice.

"Really, George! Drawing comic strips is not a proper way for a grown man to earn his living!"

Dad grinned. "Trouble is, she's got no sense of humor. Oh well, it's only for a few days. We'll just have to try not to upset her, Sam."

But not upsetting Aunt Cynthia seemed impossible. She complained that her tea was too hot, her bathwater too cold, her boiled egg too soft, and the toast too hard. When she asked what they were having for lunch, Dad said vaguely, "Oh, the usual, I expect. Bread and cheese and fruit."

Aunt Cynthia looked horrified. "No wonder you're both so skinny! While I'm staying here, you're going to eat proper meals. Samantha, take me to the grocery store. I intend to stock up your kitchen."

After lunch – delicious tuna casserole and apple pie – Aunt Cynthia fell asleep in the armchair and Dad shut himself in his den to work. By now Sam was beginning to feel fed up. She had enjoyed the tuna casserole, but she resented the way Aunt Cynthia had taken over their lives.

The doorbell rang. Aunt Cynthia didn't stir.

Sam went into the hall and flung open the front door. Jovan stood on the step, holding a large square object covered by a checkered tablecloth.

"Yes?" she said in an annoyed voice. "What do you want?"

"Hi, Sam," he said. "You sound a bit stressed."

"I'm *very* stressed," said Sam. "Aunt Cynthia's driving me crazy!"

Jovan's face fell. "I'd forgotten she was coming to stay with you."

"So it's no use asking me to do any petsitting jobs." Sam glanced at the large square object. "I don't know what you've got in there, but you'll have to take it away again. You know Aunt Cynthia hates animals."

"This isn't an animal," Jovan lifted the cloth. "It's a parrot."

Sam couldn't resist peering into the cage. "So it is! And not just any old parrot, either. It's an African Grey! They're the best kind of talking birds you can get."

Jovan dropped the cloth back over the cage. "Oh, Alfie's a talker all right."

Sam said wistfully, "I've always wanted a parrot. Who does he belong to?"

"Ryan Bates. He took him to Matthew first, but Matthew's mom didn't like him, so he and Katie brought him to me." Jovan looked embarrassed. "My mom doesn't like him, either, so I was hoping you'd look after him. I'd forgotten about your Aunt Cynthia."

Sam sighed. "I'd love to look after him, honestly I would. But—"

"It's only for a week," said Jovan. "Well, five days now. I've brought all his food and a perch for him to sit on. My mom's waiting outside in the car."

"Why doesn't she like Alfie?" asked Sam, puzzled. "I thought she was crazy about animals."

"She is." Jovan looked even more embarrassed. "But she doesn't seem to like parrots much – especially ones that talk."

"How strange," said Sam. "I can't think of anything nicer than a talking parrot."

Jovan looked hopeful. "Shall I get his stuff, then?"

Sam hesitated. Surely a parrot wouldn't upset Aunt Cynthia. It wasn't like a snake or a rat. She might even find it amusing, despite not having a sense of humor. "Oh, all right," she said.

Jovan gave her the cage and raced down the path. Seconds later he returned with the T-shaped perch on a stand and the bag of food. "There's a piece of paper inside telling you how much food to give him and everything— and some corn-on-the-cob, his favorite treat. Oh, and does Aunt Cynthia like chocolates?"

"Yes, she loves them," said Sam, surprised.

"You'd better give her these, then."
Jovan handed her an enormous gold
box tied with red ribbon. "We've eaten
some, but the bottom layer's still
complete. Thanks, Sam. Bye!"

He raced back down the path. The car
drove off quickly.

Sam closed the front door. She lifted a corner of the cloth and looked inside the cage. Alfie looked back at her with curious, light-yellow eyes.

"Hello, Alfie," she said coaxingly. "I don't know why Jo's mother didn't like you. *I* think you're beautiful."

Alfie fluffed up his feathers. "*Stupid woman*," he muttered in a cross, rasping voice. "*Get lost, ratbag.*"

Chapter 3

Pass the Parrot

"Sam?" Dad appeared in the doorway of his den. "Who was that at the door?"

Hastily she dropped the cloth back over the cage. "Uh, it was Jovan."

Dad looked puzzled. "I heard someone talking, but it didn't sound like Jovan." He pointed to the cage. "What have you got there?"

"A parrot," said Sam. "Ryan Bates asked Matthew to look after him, but Matthew's mom didn't like him, so he passed him on to Jo. But Jo's mom didn't like him, either, so he brought him here to me."

Dad grinned. "Sounds like a new game. Pass the Parrot. Why didn't anyone's mother like him?"

Sam flushed. "I think it's because he talks."

Dad looked interested. "Let me have a look at him."

Nervously Sam lifted the cloth. "His name's Alfie."

Dad bent down to peer into the cage. "Hello, Alfie. You're a fine-looking bird, I must say."

The parrot fluffed up his feathers. "*Get lost, ratbag,*" he said in his gruff, rasping voice. "*You get on my nerves.*"

Dad laughed. "That's amazing! Does he say anything else?"

"I don't know yet," Sam said. "Dad, could you please keep him in your den? I don't think Aunt Cynthia will like him very much, especially if he keeps telling her to get lost."

Dad looked around. "Where *is* the old bat?"

"Sssh!" hissed Sam. "She's still asleep in the front room."

"No, I'm not." Aunt Cynthia came into the hall, looking wide awake. "Did I hear my name?"

"*Stupid woman*," muttered Alfie. "*You get on my*—"

"Ahem, ahem!" Dad cleared his throat loudly to cover the rest of Alfie's speech. Sam dropped the cloth over the cage.

Aunt Cynthia looked puzzled. "I beg your pardon?"

Dad smiled at her. "I said hello, Aunt. Did you have a good sleep?"

"Now George, you know I never sleep in the middle of the day. I merely closed my eyes for a few minutes." She fumbled for the red-framed spectacles hanging from a chain around her neck and put them on her nose. "What have you got there?"

"Oh, just something Jovan brought for Dad." Sam thrust the cage at her father. "A prop for one of his drawings."

"A prop? What do you mean by a prop?" asked Aunt Cynthia.

"A stuffed bird," said Dad. "I need one for my new comic strip. It's called *The Rude Parrot*." He winked at Sam.

Aunt Cynthia shuddered. "A stuffed bird – how revolting! And what's that perch thing – and that bag?"

"More props." Sam picked them up and thrust them at her father. "You'd better put them away, Dad. They're making the hall look messy."

Grinning, he carried them into his den and closed the door.

Aunt Cynthia frowned. "What did George say his new comic strip was called?"

"Uh, *The Rude Parrot*," said Sam.

"Mmm." She frowned even deeper. "I don't like the sound of that at all. If there's one thing I detest, it's rudeness. It's not something to make a joke about."

Sam said quickly, "Jovan brought a present for you as well, Aunt Cynthia. It's a box of chocolates."

"For me?" Aunt Cynthia stared at the enormous gold box tied with red ribbon. "How very kind of him! I *adore* chocolates."

Sam nodded. "I told him you did."

A loud squawk came from inside the den. Aunt Cynthia looked up, startled. "What was that?"

"Uh – just Dad coughing," said Sam.

Aunt Cynthia frowned. "He should see a doctor."

"It's nothing serious," Sam said quickly. "He often coughs like that. Why don't you open the box?"

Aunt Cynthia hesitated. "I have to watch my weight, you know."

"One won't hurt you," said Sam. "Go on."

"Oh, very well." She undid the ribbon and lifted the lid. Her face fell. "Somebody's already eaten half of them!"

"Yes, I know. But Jovan said the bottom layer's still complete."

"How strange to give someone a half-eaten box of chocolates." Aunt Cynthia sighed. "Oh well, I suppose I may as well finish them off." She disappeared into the living room.

Sam opened the door of the den and looked inside. "Dad? What made Alfie squawk?"

"I let him out of his cage." Dad sat at his drawing-board, sketching away like mad. "He flew straight onto his perch and squawked with delight. I don't think he likes being stuck behind bars."

"I don't blame him." Sam went over to the perch.

Alfie certainly looked happier now that he was out of his cage. He shifted from side to side, flexing his wings and making little *brrrr brrrr* noises. Sam stroked the top of his head with a gentle finger. "Hello, Alfie," she murmured.

"*Get lost, ratbag,*" he said. "*You've got a big bottom.*"

Sam stared at him. "And you're very rude!" she exclaimed.

"That's nothing," said Dad with a grin. "You should hear some of the things he said before you came in. They even made me blush."

"*Fuss, fuss, fuss,*" said Alfie. "*You get on my nerves.*"

Sam giggled. "I wonder who taught him to say those things?"

"Whoever it was didn't like women much," said Dad.

"*Bossy old trout!*" said Alfie in a voice of deep loathing.

Dad laughed. "See what I mean? And he's an amazing mimic. Every now and then, he makes a noise like someone knocking on the door. Then he says, in quite a different voice, '*Wake up, lazybones. There's work to be done.*'"

"No wonder Ryan's mom didn't want him in the house." Sam sighed. "And now we've got him!"

"I'm not complaining." Dad went back to his drawing-board. "He makes a wonderful model."

"The trouble is, we've also got Aunt Cynthia," Sam pointed out.

"*Stupid woman!*" muttered Alfie. "*Big bottom.*"

"No problem," said Dad. "We'll just have to keep him quiet when she's around, that's all."

He made it sound so easy. But Sam couldn't help wondering how long they could keep Alfie quiet. How long before Aunt Cynthia realized there was a talking parrot in the house?

And how long before he said something really, really rude to her?

Chapter 4

A Fine Trick

Matthew felt guilty. Four days had passed since he had handed Alfie over to Jovan without telling him why his mother wouldn't have him in the house. How was Jovan getting along with the rude parrot?

He said to Katie, "I think I'll go over to Jo's house and make sure he's okay."

"I'll come, too," she said. "And I'll bring Mr. Toad so that he can see how well I'm looking after him."

But when they arrived at Jovan's house, he seemed strangely reluctant to let them in. "Sorry," he said, starting to close the door. "I'm busy right now . . . ."

"Don't you want to see Mr. Toad?" Katie held out the glass tank to show him. "He's much better. Look, he's getting very active."

The toad did a couple of feeble hops as if to prove her words. But Jovan only said, "I'll tell my dad. Bye—"

"Wait!" Matthew put his hand against the door. "We really came to ask about Alfie. How are you getting along with him?"

"Uh . . ." Jovan looked embarrassed. "Not very well, I'm afraid. At least, I liked him okay, but my mom didn't."

"Our mom didn't like him, either," said Katie. "He kept calling her ratbag and telling her she was a bossy old trout."

"He told *my* mom she had a big bottom," said Jovan. "She was furious!"

"Sorry, Jo," said Matthew. "I should have warned you. Do you want us to take him back?"

Jovan looked even more embarrassed. "Actually, I haven't got him anymore."

"Haven't *got* him?" Matthew was horrified. "You didn't let him escape?"

"No, of course not. I gave him to Sam."

"Jo!" said Katie, shocked. "We made a bargain. We said if you took Alfie, I'd look after Mr. Toad."

"Yes, I know." He looked ashamed. "Do you want me to take him back?"

"No!" She clutched the glass tank to her chest. "I love Mr. Toad. I want to go on looking after him until he's well enough to be set free."

"Thanks," said Jovan. "The trouble is, I'd forgotten Sam's Great Aunt Cynthia was coming to stay. I hope Alfie hasn't been too rude to her."

"Let's go and find out," said Matthew.

When Sam opened the door, she said, "Well! That was a fine trick you played on me!"

"Sorry, Sam," said Matthew. "But it was really Ryan Bates's trick. He said his mom had a friend coming to stay and didn't want Alfie in the house. But he didn't explain why."

"Neither did you when you passed him on to me," Jovan reminded Matthew.

"You didn't either, Jo, when you passed him on to me!" Sam pointed out.

Katie asked, "Has he been rude to your Aunt Cynthia yet?"

Before Sam could answer, Aunt Cynthia appeared in the hall behind her.

"Ah, Samantha, I see you have visitors. Your friends from school. Aren't you going to ask them in?"

Sam made a face at the Petsitters that told them clearly, GO!

"We can't stay," said Matthew. "We've got lots of jobs to do."

"He means gardening jobs," said Sam.

Aunt Cynthia didn't know about the Petsitters Club – if she did she wouldn't approve.

"We only came over to ask about Alfie," said Jovan.

"Alfie?" said Aunt Cynthia. "Who's Alfie?"

Matthew saw that Sam was still making faces, really terrible faces, as if she were trying hard to make them shut up.

But Katie hadn't noticed. "He's a parrot," she said brightly. "Jovan brought him over."

"Ah yes, I remember," said Aunt Cynthia. "The stuffed bird that George is using as a prop. He took it into his den and has been drawing it ever since. We've hardly seen him for the last three days."

Matthew, Jovan, and Katie looked puzzled. Sam mouthed silently: *She doesn't know he's alive!*

"Oh!" Matthew grinned. "The *stuffed* bird . . . !"

Katie giggled. Jovan said, "We thought he'd find it useful."

Aunt Cynthia went on, "And wasn't it also Jovan who brought me a half-eaten box of chocolates?"

Jovan looked embarrassed. "Yes, I'm sorry about that."

"Never mind, it was a very kind thought," Aunt Cynthia said graciously. "I insist you all come in and have a snack."

Matthew hesitated. Sam looked as if she was in agony.

But Katie said, "Thanks, we'd love to." Still clutching Mr. Toad's tank, she marched inside.

Chapter 5

Aunt Cynthia's Special Remedy

"Lemonade? Cake? Cookies?" asked Aunt Cynthia, bustling about the kitchen.

"Yes, please!" chorused the Petsitters.

Sam stood by the door, inwardly seething. Aunt Cynthia was doing it again! She acted as if this were *her* house instead of Sam's, handing out *her* food and *her* drink to *her* friends. Okay, so she was only being kind, but it made Sam hopping mad!

At that moment a faint squawking noise came from behind the closed door of the den. The Petsitters looked at each other in alarm. *Alfie!*

squawk!

"Tch, tch," tutted Aunt Cynthia. "I do wish George would see a doctor about that cough. It's getting worse."

Squawk! Squawk!

"That settles it!" said Aunt Cynthia. "I shall make him some of my special cough remedy. Samantha, I need a fresh lemon, honey, some soy sauce, and some cloves."

"I don't think we've got any cloves," said Sam.

"Then I'll find something else." Aunt Cynthia searched the kitchen shelves. "Ah, black pepper. That will do nicely."

She carried the bottles and jars over to the table and set to work, watched in silence by the Petsitters. First she mixed all the ingredients together in a pitcher and stirred them vigorously. Then she tasted it, frowned, and went to the cupboard for more ingredients.

"It's a very strange color," said Sam, watching her stir them in.

"It doesn't matter what it looks like as long as it works." Aunt Cynthia poured some into a glass. "My special remedy cures everything, not only coughs. You'll see."

She carried the empty bottles and jars back to the sink. While her back was turned, Katie picked up the glass and poured some of the mixture into Mr. Toad's water bowl.

Aunt Cynthia turned around. She stared at Katie in astonishment. "What are you doing?" she demanded.

"You said your special remedy cured everything," said Katie. "I thought perhaps it might cure Mr. Toad."

Aunt Cynthia put on her spectacles and peered into the tank. "Ugh, what an ugly creature!"

"He's not ugly," Katie said indignantly. "He's beautiful!"

Aunt Cynthia gave her a stern look. "Toads do not belong in kitchens. What if he jumped out and got mixed up with the food? Most unhygienic."

"He's too sick to jump out," Katie said. "I'm nursing him until he's better."

"That's beside the point. Kindly remove him at once."

"I'll put him in the hall," Katie said meekly.

Aunt Cynthia picked up the glass. "Now I shall take this to George."

"No!" said Sam quickly. "No, you can't go into his den."

"Why ever not?"

Sam flushed. "He – he doesn't like being disturbed. I never interrupt him when he's working."

Squawk, squawk!

"Did you hear that?" Aunt Cynthia demanded. "He's coughing again. No time to lose."

She marched out of the kitchen.

Sam and the others looked at one another. "We've got to stop her!" said Sam. "Come on."

They followed Aunt Cynthia into the hall just in time to see her knock on the door of the den. "George, may I come in? I've brought you some of my special cough remedy."

"Wait a minute," came Dad's muffled voice.

Aunt Cynthia waited impatiently for about five seconds. Then she opened the door and marched in.

Sam and the others crowded into the room behind her. Dad stood in front of the table, looking flustered – but where was Alfie? His perch was empty, and there was no sign of the cage.

"Drink this, George." Aunt Cynthia held out the glass.

Dad didn't move.

"Take it," she urged. "It'll do you good."

Reluctantly Dad took a step toward her – revealing the parrot's cage standing on the table behind him, with Alfie inside! Sam guessed at once what had happened. When Dad heard Aunt Cynthia knock on the door, he must have lifted the parrot from his perch and hastily shoved him into the cage. The trouble was, he hadn't had time to cover it with the cloth.

He stared at the cough remedy. "What's in it?"

"All sorts of things," said Sam, watching Alfie out of the corner of her eye. Luckily he was sitting still. In fact, he looked exactly like a stuffed bird.

"Like what?" Dad asked suspiciously.

"Like honey and lemon and pepper," said Matthew. He, too, was watching Alfie.

"And soy sauce," said Katie.

"And some other stuff we didn't see," added Jovan.

Dad sniffed at the khaki-colored mixture. "Aunt, I don't really need this. . . ."

But at that moment, Alfie opened his beak and uttered a loud "*SQUAWK!*"

Hastily Matthew moved to stand in front of the table, masking the cage. Dad covered his mouth with his hand, as if it were he who had made the noise.

"Clearly you *do* need it, George!" commanded Aunt Cynthia. "Drink up."

He took a sip and nearly choked. "It's disgusting!"

"Of course it's disgusting," she agreed. "Medicine has to be disgusting, otherwise it doesn't do you any good. Drink it down and don't be such a baby."

Dad closed his eyes and took another sip. At the same moment, a voice spoke from behind Matthew.

"*Fuss, fuss, fuss. Stupid woman!*"

Everyone froze.

Chapter 6

Bossy Old Trout

"Who said that?" demanded Aunt Cynthia.

"Get lost, ratbag!"

Aunt Cynthia looked around at each of them in turn. When she came to Matthew, her eyes narrowed. "Was that you, young man?"

Matthew opened his mouth to speak,

but no sound came out. Instead there came a voice from behind him:

"*Bossy old trout. You get on my nerves.*"

Aunt Cynthia gasped. "How dare you! You – you – you rude boy!"

Sam said quickly, "It wasn't Matthew, Aunt Cynthia, honestly it wasn't."

"Well, if it wasn't him, who was it?" She glared first at Sam, then Jovan, then Katie. "Come on, own up!"

Silence. Then: "*You've got a big bottom!*"

Aunt Cynthia's eyes nearly popped out of her head. She turned very, very red.

Then she turned very, very white. She said faintly, "I have never been so insulted in my life!"

Sam felt terrible. All the Petsitters looked uncomfortable.

Then Dad said, "Sorry, Aunt. It wasn't any of them, it was me."

She stared at him. "Don't be silly, George. It couldn't possibly have been you. The voice came from somewhere else entirely."

"Ah, that's because I'm a – a ventriloquist," said Dad. "I can throw my voice to the other side of the room if I want to. I've been practicing lately, and I've become really good at it. Haven't I, Sam?"

Sam didn't know what to say. "Uh – yes," she muttered.

Aunt Cynthia said, "But – but I was looking straight at you, George! You were drinking down my cough remedy. . . ."

"Oh, that's a very old trick," Dad said confidently. "All ventriloquists can drink a glass of water and talk at the same time. It's easy once you know how."

"*Bossy old trout, big bottom!*"

"You see?" said Dad, triumphant. "I did it again."

"But – but – but, George . . ." Aunt Cynthia looked stunned. "Is that really what you think of me, that I'm a bossy old trout with a big bottom?"

Sam groaned inwardly. Now they were in trouble!

Dad saw the trap he had fallen into. "No, of course not! It's just a saying I use in my ventriloquist act. Get lost, ratbag – it makes people laugh. I wasn't talking about *you*, Aunt."

But Aunt Cynthia didn't seem to hear him. "It's true I've put on some weight lately," she said unhappily. "I shouldn't have eaten those chocolates."

"You haven't put on any weight," Sam assured her. "Honestly, you look fine."

"Then why did your father say I had a big bottom?"

"He didn't mean it." She appealed to her father. "Did you, Dad?"

"No, of course not," said Dad. "I was just making a joke."

"A very *cruel* joke." Aunt Cynthia sounded close to tears. "I think I'll go upstairs, if you don't mind. I'd like to be alone for a while."

They were all silent as she left the room.

Then Sam said, "Oh Dad, how *could* you! Poor Aunt Cynthia, she's really upset."

He groaned. "I didn't mean to hurt her feelings. I was only trying to keep the rest of you from getting into trouble."

"*Fuss, fuss, fuss!*" squawked Alfie. "*Stupid woman.*"

Everyone turned to glare at him. "It's *your* fault, Alfie," Matthew said accusingly. "You're the one who's caused all the trouble."

"It's no use blaming Alfie," said Dad. "He only repeats what he's been taught. And he doesn't like being closed up in his cage." He opened the door. Alfie hopped out onto his hand, making happy little *brrr brrr* noises.

"He seems to like you, Dad," said Sam.

"We've become good friends," said Dad. "He flies around the room and sits on my shoulder when I'm working. All he needs is human company and lots of attention."

Jovan nodded. "My dad says that's what all parrots need. They get really distressed if people ignore them."

"I guess Aunt Cynthia's feeling pretty distressed right now," said Sam. "She's a nice old lady, really. After all, she only fusses because she cares. I'd better go up and tell her the truth."

Dad sighed. "Poor Aunt Cynthia. Tell her I'm very, very sorry, and try to make her understand."

"I'll do my best," Sam promised.

She left the room.

Chapter 7

Hello, Gorgeous!

The bedroom door stood slightly open. Sam knocked gently. "Aunt Cynthia? May I come in?"

No reply.

Sam peered around the door. To her dismay she saw an open suitcase on the bed. "You're not leaving!"

"Indeed I am." Aunt Cynthia took a

dress from the closet and folded it into the case. "George doesn't want me here. The sooner I go, the better."

"No, you're wrong!" Sam ventured farther into the room. "He wants you to stay."

Aunt Cynthia shook her head. "He thinks I fuss too much and try to interfere." She fumbled for a handkerchief and dabbed her eyes. "You heard what he called me – a bossy old trout."

"But that wasn't Dad speaking," said Sam. "It was Alfie."

"Don't be silly, Samantha. How can a stuffed parrot speak?"

"Because he isn't stuffed. He's alive."

"Alive?" Aunt Cynthia stared at her. "You told me it was a prop!"

"I wasn't telling the truth." Sam took a deep breath. "We're looking after him for somebody – me and Matthew and Jovan and Katie. That's what we do.

We're petsitters, not gardeners. I didn't dare tell you before because I know you don't like animals."

"Petsitters?"

"Matthew was standing in front of Alfie's cage—that's why you thought it was him speaking. Dad only pretended he was a ventriloquist to keep Matthew from getting into trouble."

"A talking parrot . . . ," Aunt Cynthia murmured thoughtfully.

"And when you thought Dad was coughing, it was really Alfie squawking. That's why Dad didn't want to drink your special remedy."

"I see." Aunt Cynthia sighed. "But it's true, isn't it? I *am* a bossy old trout at times. And I fuss too much, I know I do."

"Yes, but only because you worry about us not eating properly and living in a messy house," Sam pointed out.

"I expect it's because I live alone and am used to doing things my own way. But I will try to stop, I promise." Aunt Cynthia blew her nose and stuffed the handkerchief up her sleeve. Bravely she attempted a smile. "A talking parrot? Well, I never!"

"Alfie's a nice bird, really," Sam said. "Would you like to come downstairs and meet him properly?"

Aunt Cynthia hesitated. Then she said, "Oh, very well. Why not?"

"And you will stay, won't you?" asked Sam anxiously.

"If you insist." Aunt Cynthia braced her shoulders. "I think you'd better tell me all about this petsitting business."

They went downstairs. In the hall they met Katie, holding the glass tank.

"Mr. Toad's feeling better," she said. "Look . . ."

Aunt Cynthia peered into the tank. "How can you tell? He's not moving around—"

At that moment Mr. Toad leaped into the air, almost hitting Aunt Cynthia on the nose. She jumped back in alarm.

Sam held her breath. Was Aunt Cynthia going to be angry?

Katie said quickly, "I guess it was your special remedy that cured him. Now we'll be able to set him free."

Aunt Cynthia looked pleased. "Well, I'm glad that *somebody* appreciates my special remedy!" She drew a deep breath. "And if I can cure a toad, I can certainly cope with a rude parrot!"

They entered the den to find Alfie perched on Dad's shoulder. When he saw Aunt Cynthia, he fluffed up his feathers and made a loud squawking noise.

"Good heavens!" she exclaimed. "He really *is* a live parrot!"

"Hello, Aunt," said Dad. "Did Sam explain . . . ?"

"Samantha has explained everything," said Aunt Cynthia. "And don't worry, George. From now on I shall never behave like a bossy old trout again."

Dad grinned and kissed her on the cheek. "I don't care how bossy you are, you're still my favorite aunt. And Alfie doesn't mean to be rude, you know. He's only repeating what he's been taught to say."

Aunt Cynthia gave him a gracious nod. "I realize that. And he's quite a handsome bird, when you look at him properly." She gazed up at Alfie and put on a wheedling voice. "Who's a pretty boy, then?"

Alfie fluffed up his feathers and preened himself. "*Hello, gorgeous!*" he said.

Later Sam tackled her father in private. "He's never said that before. And he spoke in *your* voice! Did you teach it to him?"

Dad grinned. "I've just spent three whole days shut up in my den with that bird. It seemed like a good idea to teach him how to be more polite. Mind you, that was the first time he'd ever actually *said* it. He has excellent timing."

Sam gave Alfie a piece of corn-on-the-cob as a reward. "Aunt Cynthia really likes him now," she said. "I think she'll be sorry to see him go."

"So will I," said Dad, then groaned as Alfie spat out bits of corn all over his drawing board. "Although he does have some very messy habits."

"*Fuss, fuss, fuss,*" said Alfie. Suddenly he made a knocking sound, as if someone were at the door. "*Wake up, lazybones,*" he said in a sharp, high voice, quite different from his usual gruff tones. "*There's work to be done.*"

Dad grinned. "You know, I can't help wondering who taught him to say all those things – and why."

Sam wondered, too. When Matthew brought Ryan over to pick up Alfie, she asked him to explain.

"Alfie belonged to my dad's old uncle," Ryan told her. "Uncle Spencer was scared to death of his wife. She was a big, bossy woman who wouldn't let him bring his parrot into the house, so he kept Alfie in the garden shed and taught him to say all the things he wasn't brave enough to say himself. When he died he left some money to my dad in his will on the condition that he give Alfie a good home. He said Alfie had been his best friend."

"Poor Uncle Spencer," said Sam. "So when Alfie uses that high voice, he must be imitating the wife. I expect she often knocked on the shed door and told him there was work to be done. No wonder he called her a bossy old trout!"

Matthew grinned. "She sounds even worse than Sam's Aunt Cynthia."

"Oh, Aunt Cynthia's okay, really." Sam stroked the parrot's head. "I shall miss you, Alfie – and so will Dad. But you will try to be more polite in the future, won't you?"

Alfie fluffed up his feathers. "*Get lost, ratbag*," he told her sternly.

The End